KATHERINE SPARACINO

WestBow Press books may be ordered through booksellers or by contacting:

WestBow Press
A Division of Thomas Nelson & Zondervan
1663 Liberty Drive
Bloomington, IN 47403
www.westbowpress.com
844-714-3454

Cover art by Rosemary Ranck

ISBN: 978-1-6642-6779-4 (sc)
ISBN: 978-1-6642-6778-7 (e)

Print information available on the last page.

WestBow Press rev. date: 6/29/2022

Dedicated to my Aunt Peggy, smiling down
from Heaven at my accomplishment

CONTENTS

Chapter 1

WILD HORSES

REBECCA and Falling Rock left at sunrise on their packed horses: Rebecca on her palomino filly, *Columbine,* and Falling Rock on his Appaloosa stallion *Cloud.*

"It's a bit chilly." Rebecca shivered in her jacket.

"Sun will warm you." Falling Rock pointed to the yellow glow on treetops as they rode east.

The sky opened up revealing range upon range of mountaintops on the horizon, many still white with snow. "My goodness," Rebecca gasped, "I had no idea there were so many!"

"Little valley where we live not show much mountains, must go higher to see."

Songbirds awakened with the sunrise, as did ground squirrels that chased each other in and out of the trees. At least they were smart enough to stay away from the horses' hooves.

Following game trails, they rode close to the forest edge. Rebecca removed her jacket and cinched her hat to shade the sun's glare. "How much farther?"

"Soon. Need rest?"

Columbine showed no signs of fatigue. Rebecca stroked her mane. “No we can go on.”

They turned into woodland and began ascending a steep incline. The horses became edgy and snorted. “What’s wrong?” Rebecca asked.

“Hear thunder sound.”

“But it’s a clear day.” They came into a meadow carpeted with various types of wildflowers nodding in the breeze, a rainbow of brilliant colors in splendor. The ground shook as the sound got closer. Rebecca was alarmed. “What is it?”

“Look!” Falling Rock pointed to a stampeding herd of wild horses crossing a river ahead of them. Columbine and Cloud struggled and reared trying to get free. Their riders held on tight maintaining control.

“I’ve never seen such a sight! How beautiful they are!” Rebecca stared in amazement as she tried to quiet her horse. “Wow! If we could catch some of them, they would really help our operation of supplying horses to people who need them.”

Falling Rock adamantly shook his head. “Wild, no catch, must stay free.”

Rebecca knew that if anyone else found them they would be caught, but she didn’t argue. Once they passed, their horses calmed down.

As the dust settled, Falling Rock followed the path of the animals. Rebecca heard another sound, a waterfall; she saw it before she noticed the pool it cascaded into.

“This place,” Falling Rock explained, “I discover many moons ago and tell no one. I not come here since.”

Rebecca had no words. She was in awe. The white water rushed into an aqua pool. She inhaled deeply. They climbed down and began unpacking the horses.

Captain Jerry Anderson led his men up the narrow, rugged trail through the mountains. He was sure he could find renegade Indians to take back to the fort. The men didn't dare complain about the route or the mission.

When they reached the top, Anderson scanned the area with field glasses, and let out a disgruntled sigh. "Let's rest here, men, and then we'll go on."

They walked the horses to cool them down, picketed and watered them. The men spread out under the trees. Two sat together on a rock with their canteens. "I wonder how much longer we're going to do this."

"Who knows? He seems obsessed about it. I thought all the Indians were rounded up in 1881, four years ago."

"Men!" the captain shouted. "We'll finish this patrol and then go back to the fort!"

The next morning as Rebecca and Falling Rock headed for home, a scout from Anderson's unit reported back to him.

"An Indian, sir, riding with a white girl, just up ahead."

"This is it, men. Load your weapons and prepare for a fight."

"Stop!" Captain Anderson shouted as they came near.

Rebecca turned to see the soldiers. "Oh my!"

They circled the couple with guns drawn.

"What's this?" Rebecca demanded.

"We're scouting for renegades, ma'am, and looks like we found one."

"Falling Rock is no renegade!"

"Are you sure you're not a brainwashed white captive?"

"I never heard of such a thing! I am Rebecca Ruth MacKenzie. Falling Rock is my husband, and he works on our ranch in Maysville."

"Do you have identification that states this?"

"Come to my house, and my father will explain everything."

"I've been to Maysville," Captain Anderson snarled. "I was told there were protected Indians there." He sat up high in his saddle. "But you're not on your ranch now. Men, secure him!"

The soldiers took the reins from Falling Rock and tied his hands behind his back.

"You can't do this!" Rebecca shrieked.

"Ma'am, you can explain this to Major Oxford at the newly established army base, Fort Logan, in Denver." Captain Anderson tipped his hat and they rode away.

"No!" Rebecca howled. Falling Rock turned to look at her, just as one of the soldiers struck his face, knocking him to the ground. They forced him to walk away.

Chapter 2

DEFENSE

JOEL MacKenzie, along with Rebecca and Frederick traveled to Denver, where they hired their attorney, Rueben Marston. Marston had previously declared the Indian Charter of 1867 legal. Together, they proceeded to Fort Logan.

Shackled and bruised, Falling Rock was led into the room and seated at the end of a long table with Frederick and Marston. They talked for a few minutes before Major Oxford waddled in.

Oxford was large, stretching his uniform, having white hair, a moustache and short beard. He sat at the other end of the table in an overstuffed chair, with Major Anderson's report in his hand. Rebecca and Joel sat across the room, looking nervously at each other, in front of Anderson, was seated behind them.

"You may begin," Oxford said.

Marston stood up. "We live in a land of contradictions where *all men are created equal* yet slaves were bought and sold, and Indians are herded like cattle onto reservations. They have become a pathetic people who drag out a wretched existence as best they can on the miserable pittance doled out to them. It seems the promise of personal freedom, guaranteed by the Constitution, is given to those who already have it.

"Falling Rock was born free in a land where he could live, have food, make clothes, and take care of his people. It was others who made decisions to remove him from his indigenous and autonomous lifestyle.

"A charter was drawn up in 1867 by the MacKenzie family to house and protect the survivors of a vicious attack upon them by renegade white men. This is a copy of it." Marston handed the document to Oxford. "On this ranch they are allowed to work, and children go to school learning the English language and American law.

"Falling Rock has prepared his own defense. Frederick MacKenzie will translate his words." Marston sat down while Frederick stood up and said:

"You say you are men of principle and truth who uphold the laws of God and man for the cause of freedom. Yet you drag me away from my family and treat me worse than the animals I care for. You call me and my people savages, yet the only savagery I've seen is from rebel white men who came and killed my people and destroyed the places that we lived and hunted. I was born where horses run free, and I was taken away from there."

A long silence filled the room as Major Oxford thought about these words and studied the documents. "I will need to confer with a higher authority," he finally said.

"Can Falling Rock be released and come home?" Marston asked.

"What will prevent him from running away?"

Falling Rock stood up. "No run. Go home to ranch."

"Major," Marston stated, "you can release Falling Rock into the custody of Joel MacKenzie, who will be responsible for his safekeeping."

"We will take a recess while this is considered."

A guard walked Falling Rock back to jail. When they passed Rebecca, she reached out to embrace him, but the soldier pushed her back. He then yanked on Falling Rock's chains.

"This has gone on far enough!" Joel told Marston, who cautioned him to sit down and be quiet.

Major Oxford lumbered in to the front of the room with a telegram in his hand. "I have conferred with Major General William W. Allen by telegraph. It is not my position to make, or change, government policies. That is for the lawmakers in Washington. It *is* the directive of the Bureau of Indian Affairs, along with the army, to quell hostile situations and arrest those renegades who have left reservations and cause unrest.

"This doesn't seem to be the case with Falling Rock. He's never been on a reservation, nor is there any evidence of aggressive behavior. Therefore, I will abide by the original charter and allow Falling Rock to be released to the MacKenzies and returned to his home.

"He is not to leave MacKenzie property again without proper identification. This hearing is closed."

Captain Anderson's countenance stiffened and his eyes narrowed with anger as he glared at Falling Rock.

A clerk wrote on an Identification Card: "Falling Rock, Arapaho Indian, works and resides at the MacKenzie Ranch in Maysville, Colorado."

Chapter 3

THE GREAT SPIRIT

REBECCA and Falling Rock were in the corral training a young colt. They were gently talking to it while stroking his mane and head. Holding the lead rope, which was attached to the halter, they backed away and Rebecca climbed up on the fence. Falling Rock kept eye contact and the horse began to walk.

"What is the Great Spirit?" she asked.

"Great Spirit make all things: earth, sky, clouds; make animals and man. Teach us to live with all. We are one with – " He stopped, not knowing the word.

"Nature?" Rebecca suggested.

"Yes, nature. We learn from animals, we see signs for help with life."

"Your life is in constant contact with the Great Spirit. You live simply."

Falling Rock nodded. "All that we see around us are blessings. White man struggle with nature, destroy earth. Fight and swallow each other.

"Nature helps us understand better. It puts senses in order, to be soothed and healed. Away from nature, man's heart becomes hard. People need beauty and bread, places to pray and play. Nature heal and give strength to body and soul – find sacred silence."

Rebecca stared in amazement at his wisdom. "But, your people practiced *raiding*, didn't they?"

"Yes," he nodded. His face became sad. "Indians do many bad things: have wars, fight, kill. We had enemies. We took from others. I no like that. My people come here to live in peace."

"Until we came," she sighed.

"Not you! Others!" He was stern. "We talk before!"

"You're right!" She took a deep breath. "People can be evil."

"But much good in world: love, children."

"Yes, we need to look for the good." She tossed her red hair and replaced her hat.

Falling Rock intensified his eye contact, which encouraged the horse to begin to trot. "What you think of Great Spirit?"

"Our Bible says the Spirit of God created the heavens and the earth. Our God is also a Great Spirit." She watched the colt circle the ring. "Your English is much better now. Maybe you should learn how to read. The children are doing very well in school."

"No need to read. Great Spirit teach all."

"But reading would help you learn how to interact better with white man."

"I do fine with family."

She knew he wanted no further interaction with outsiders, so she gave up the discussion for the time being.

On their one-year anniversary, Rebecca remembered the events leading up to this day:

She had dragged her grandmother's trunk out from under her bed and was startled when she saw Butterfly's tack inside. She mourned the loss of her horse for a few moments. Then she placed the tack and her journal on her desk, and began sifting through the contents. At the very bottom, wrapped in canvas, was her mother's wedding dress. She carefully lifted the bundle and spread it out on her bed as her mother came in.

"What's this?" Ruth asked.

"I've been thinking for a long time about marrying Falling Rock."

"I knew this day would come," Ruth said. "Does he agree with this?"

"Yes, we talk about love and children; and we talk about the Great Spirit. He believes the Indian lives with nature; I also think that's a better way of life."

Ruth only nodded as she helped Rebecca unwrap the dress. "My mother made this for me when I married your father. I'm pleased that you want to wear it." Once the garment was on, Ruth commented, "We're going to have to take it up quite a bit. You're such a short, little thing." The women laughed and hugged each other.

Upon shortening the skirt, there was enough material to make Rising Moon a little dress too.

All of the residents of the MacKenzie Ranch had gathered in the yard at sundown for the wedding. Running Fox, a survivor of the attack on the Indians, shared the Indian concepts of intention, commitment, community, and harmony, and gave a blessing to all present.

Falling Rock and Rebecca washed each other's hands in a basin on a stand as a cleansing symbolizing purity.

Reverend Graham Tucker spoke Christian words regarding marriage, sacrifice, and duty, and blessed the union in the name of the Father, Son, and Holy Ghost. He also wrote the certificate of marriage in Rebecca's Bible.

The Indian women hosted a celebration, assisted by Ruth and May, with native dancing and food. Rebecca danced with her father.

"I'm so proud of you," Joel said. "You stuck by your principles of treating the Indians as human beings. Falling Rock is a good man and will take care of you."

"Most likely I'll probably be taking care of him," she laughed.

"Yes. That's how it's supposed to be."

Falling Rock came to carry Rebecca to his cabin as the party continued until midnight.

Chapter 4

CAMPING

ANDREW and Burning Bear, both 17, enjoyed going camping. To Burning Bear it was like old times, living off the land again. They hiked up the rocky east fork of Clear Creek to the open meadow where Frederick first met Falling Rock. Along the way they saw bighorn sheep rustling among the trees.

"This looks like a good place," Andrew said, as they approached level ground.

The brown grass was clipped short due to the feeding habits of several animals. Autumn flowers were in bloom, mostly yellow daisies and orange sunflowers, heavy with seeds.

"Our people stayed here many times. There was more game then, not so much now. But look-" Burning Bear pointed to three moose in the wetlands along the forest edge.

"Wow. That's a big, old buck. We'd better stay away from him!"

They collected stones to make a fire ring, and spread their blankets on the ground. Andrew tried to speak in Burning Bear's native tongue. "This place sure is beautiful."

Burning Bear rolled his head, groaning.

"What did I say?"

"The sky is hungry." They both laughed and wrestled on the ground until they were breathless.

They searched among the trees for firewood; Burning Bear showed Andrew places where his people had been sharpening arrowheads. They found pieces of broken pottery used in collecting berries. Andrew began picking up the arrowheads. Burning Bear put his hand on his arm, shaking his head *no.*

"Someone else may find them," Andrew explained, "and then they'll be lost forever. This way, *you* can keep them." They found a spear point and a baby's moccasin that had deteriorated some by the weather.

As dusk drifted into nightfall, the boys built a fire and broiled some venison that they had brought with them. The dripping juices sizzled and sparked on the coals as tiny flames flashed upward in their short lives.

"I think I like your sister," Burning Bear said suddenly.

"Sarah?" Burning Bear nodded. "She's nothing but a cry-baby girl, and she wants to stay in the house all the time."

Burning Bear dropped the subject.

They shared apples, something new Uncle Joe had brought into his store, then lay down mesmerized by the dying flames and rising smoke. The moonless night unfolded to a vast expanse of brilliant lights. Burning Bear showed Andrew constellations by the Indian names; Andrew didn't know them in English. They counted wandering stars streaking across the black sky until sleep enveloped them.

Andrew heard a sound and awoke with a shiver. He realized he was cold, and noticed the coals were ashen. Pulling up his coat collar, and adjusting his knitted hat, he tried to roll up in his blanket when he heard the sound again. He looked at Burning Bear who was still sleeping.

He nudged his friend until he muttered and the howling came again. "What is it?" Andrew whispered.

"Coyotes," Burning Bear mumbled.

"Are you sure it isn't wolves?"

"No, they stay up high in the summer."

Andrew lay awake wondering what the coyotes were howling about, since there was no moon, until he drifted back to sleep.

The boys continued their hike the next morning, not looking for anything in particular. Further up the trail, they did find the evidence the coyotes' presence. The soil was disturbed and bloody, animal bones littered the area.

"Looks like they feasted on a fawn last night," Burning Bear observed.

"Oh, the poor thing."

"It's the way of nature. Happens all the time. Look here." He showed Andrew a leg bone. "He had a broken leg. It couldn't go on anyway."

They continued up the mountain until they came to a great waterfall. As they stood at the base looking up, Andrew said, "My aunt Rebecca saw this waterfall when she went to Falling Rock's camp and described it to us."

"The water flow is low now since it's near the end of summer."

"It looks like it comes right out of that rock!" Andrew observed.

"There's a cave up there. The water goes into the cave and back out again."

"I'd sure like to see that! Can we go up there?"

"Yes. We'll just have to climb along the edge here." Burning Bear led the way.

The steep climb was difficult over rocks; they were unstable because the soil was damp from the splashing water. Andrew slipped on loose gravel and lost his balance, but Burning Bear caught his hand and pulled him up. When they reached the top, Andrew was breathless. "Thanks."

They stood looking at the mouth of the cave watching the water flow in. "I wonder if there's anything else in there," Andrew speculated. He envisioned the walls covered in gold.

"Let's take a look." Burning Bear picked up a dry, leafy branch and lit it for a torch with a piece of flint he always carried.

As they peered inside, they saw something white sticking out of the water. "What's that?" Andrew pointed, alarmed.

Burning Bear stepped near the edge holding up the torch. "It's a bone! Looks like a human skull. I can see another just under the water line."

"Let's get out of here!" Andrew turned to start back down. Burning Bear threw the torch into the water and followed him.

Once down the steep part, Andrew said, "My uncle Daniel told me about two prospectors, who were lost up in the mountains. That' s before your tribe was attacked. There was a search party, but no trace of them was ever found."

Burning Bear didn't comment. Andrew thought that maybe he was holding back. Either he didn't know about it, or he did know, but didn't want to say. So he let it go.

It only took a half hour to hurry down the mountain. Daniel's office was near the trail, and Andrew told him about the cave and skulls. Then he and Burning Bear ran through town to the big house and forgot about it.

Chapter 5

DREAMS

REBECCA suffered troubling dreams about their long trip west:

The temperature was searing! Rebecca's red hair was tucked up inside her white Stetson hat. Sweat ran down her back and trickled on her face. The split riding-skirt she wore shaded her legs, but inside her boots her feet were hot. She took a small sip from her canteen since water had to be rationed now, but she was still thirsty. She felt worse for her horse, Butterfly, showing signs of fatigue and drooping her head.

A rider came up alongside her; it was Jonathan. "How are you doing?"

"I can hardly bear this heat. Butterfly is suffering, too."

"I found a small pebble to help keep my mouth moist," he showed it to her between his teeth, a round piece of quartz, "but I thought you might like this instead." Reaching inside his vest he pulled out a paper bag and handed it to her.

"Boiled candy!" Rebecca squealed with delight. "Where did you find it?" She selected a red one and handed the bag back to him.

"Keep it." He smiled broadly as she popped the treat into her mouth and mumbled, "thank you."

He tipped his hat, and rode off into the dust.

"What was that all about?" Papa asked, coming up from behind on his horse.

"Oh, nothing." She was sassy. "Aren't you riding in the wagon with Mama?"

"No, May wanted a break from the sun, and she's taking a nap with Andrew. I think your mother is asleep too."

"Good for them." *I sure would like to be taking a nap right now!*

"I had Jonathan ride up ahead to see if there are any trees along this riverbed, besides these stumpy bushes. Even the creek water's almost dried up. We've got to rest these horses soon."

"I hope he does find some shade." She carefully sucked her candy, in hopes of making it last longer.

Jonathan located a stand of trees with enough shade for the horses; the wagons encircled them. Rebecca, Jonathan, and the two ranch hands, Abe and Stan, began loosening the cinches on the saddles. Once cooled down, they were led to the shallow water.

Daniel argued with his father. "We need to stop now, we're risking heat stroke for the animals and ourselves."

"But it's only noon. We could make another five miles."

"Won't do us any good if we're all dead!" He climbed into his wagon to check on his mother. "How are you feeling?"

May was wiping Ruth's face with a cloth out of a small basin of water. Ma was awake. "As good as I can be, I guess." She made an effort to stifle a cough.

"I'm trying to talk Pa into stopping here. The animals are suffering."

Tired of the jostling, but not complaining, Ruth said weakly, "That would be nice."

Daniel went to Rebecca, and told her to start unhitching the horses and removing their tack. "It's just too hot to go on."

Heat waves rose off the prairie as the family struggled to set up camp. As the sun moved around the trees, they had to keep shifting the horses' positions to keep them in the shade. "Look," Matthew told Frederick," I think I see a raincloud out there."

Frederick squinted his eyes, and tried to look where his brother was pointing, "Maybe."

Joel asked Ruth if she wanted to get out of the wagon, and sit in the rocker. "Perhaps, when the sun goes down."

An unexpected darkness blanketed the entire sky, and the wind roared. Horses whinnied and jumped, but were tied fast to the wagons and trees. Purple lightning flashed against threatening clouds; the thunder that followed was instantaneous. In a moment everything was drenched. The women climbed into the wagons, while the men opened the barrels to collect the rainwater.

Inside lanterns were being lit. The canvas wagon covers, treated with oil, kept everything dry. Joel, May and Andrew closed up the end flaps on their wagon. May was glad for the rest, as her pregnancy was becoming uncomfortable. Rebecca sat with Matthew and Frederick, Daniel stayed with Ma and Pa, and the ranch hands occupied the 4th wagon.

The wind rocked the Conestogas, which had been lashed together. The frantic horses tried to run, but couldn't get away. The temperature dropped, and hail began pounding on the wagon covers.

"My poor Butterfly," cried Rebecca. She tried to get out of the wagon, but her brother stopped her.

"You can't go out there," Matthew shouted over the noise.

"You'll get killed," Frederick added.

"But Butterfly may get killed," she bawled.

The tumult soon stopped, and everything became still. The air was cooler, but felt heavy.

Matthew peeked out of the tent. "Oh Lord! Everybody pray," he shouted. "A tornado is coming!"

The wind grew stronger again, all the MacKenzies in each wagon prayed. Then, just as the twister approached them, it turned and headed away while dissipating.

A few minutes of hushed waiting and folks started coming out of the wagons. The sun was lower and softer. Rebecca stepped in icy mud. *First it was too hot, and then there's too much rain!* She complained to herself while slogging through the mire to get to her horse.

"Oh, my dear Butterfly," she cooed while stroking her wet mane. "I'm so sorry you don't have a stall, but you will, as soon as we find the land. It's okay now." Rebecca started shaking.

"Wake up, Rebecca." She opened her eyes to see Falling Rock's smile. "You dream of Butterfly."

The realization shocked her and she began to cry. Her husband cradled her in his arms. She was afraid to go back to sleep, fearing another harsh memory. Falling Rock sang softly to her in his native tongue until she lay still and dreamed again:

The water barrels were full, but as the hail melted, the mud grew thicker and stickier. It was impossible to get the wagons moving.

"I guess we'll have to stay here," Joel grumbled. "It won't do any good to try going on until morning."

No camp was set up, as everyone stayed in their own wagon that night. Rebecca, Jonathan, and the ranch hands cared for the horses, brushing out the coats and manes. Matthew and Frederick built a stone fire pit, and cooked up some hot food.

Joel shared warm broth with Ruth. "How are you feeling?"

"Just tired." *Tired of what? The trip? The weather? This whole exploit?*

"You seem to be coughing less," he tried to encourage her.

"I suppose," she sighed, and sipped the broth. *It's all my fault we're stuck out here,* but she never said a word out loud.

The next morning Joel was annoyed. "We've got to get out of this mud," he ordered, "before it hardens and we're stuck here forever."

The horses were harnessed to the wagons, but pulling them was futile. Their hoofs would bog down in the mire.

Jonathan came up with an idea. "Let's cut these small branches and trees, and try making a path for them to walk on."

It was almost noon before they could get underway. Wheels had to be dug out first, then the paths made. The mud was drying on the wood, the sun getting hot. Men pushed the wagons from behind, while the women encouraged the horses. Rebecca used the lead rope, and walked in front of Butterfly.

Once the wagons were moving, they continued on slowly until they found some firm, dry grassland. There they set up camp.

Rebecca awoke, and realized she had just read this in her journal that day. But why was she having these dreams of being on the trail? It was when Jonathan was being nice to her. She decided to talk to her mother about it.

"Remember, darling," Ruth's soothing voice calmed her nervousness, "during that time you did like Jonathan. Now that he's gone, it's still in your memory."

"But I love Falling Rock! I don't want to think about Jonathan."

"Didn't you just read about him in your journal?"

Rebecca nodded. "I guess that brought up the memories of him." She sat for a moment digesting this. "Thanks Ma," she stood up and kissed her.

"And remember, your body is changing. You may realize other strange things too."

Chapter 6

NEWS

"LET'S sleep out under the stars tonight," Rebecca suggested to Falling Rock, as she pulled the quilt off the bed. He helped her spread it on the ground behind their cabin.

They laid still for a while, holding hands, watching lazy clouds drift past the moon, as its beams danced across the cliffs. "I've been having bad dreams."

"Yes."

"I'm dreaming about being on the trail, when we were coming out here." She paused. "And I've been dreaming about Jonathan."

"You were close."

"But I *love you!*" She turned and faced him.

He looked at her earnest expression, and kissed her.

"I don't know why I'm having these dreams now."

He touched her tummy. "Baby growing, body change."

She sat up. "What? How did you know?"

"Great Spirit tell me." He pulled her back down. "I see dancing in eyes, glow on face. I know."

"I was going to tell you tonight."

May MacKenzie was spring cleaning her apartment above the store, removing old newspapers used as insulation in the walls, and replacing them with fresh ones, when she came upon this article appearing in an 1888 newspaper: *The Purpose of Indian Schools*

> "A major objective of Indian Schools is to wean the student from the degrading communism [sic] of the tribal reservation system and imbue them with the exalting egotism of American civilization so that he will say "I" instead of "we" and "this is mine" instead of "this is ours." We need to awaken in him wants. *He must be touched by the wings of the divine angle of discontent.* Then he will begin to reach out with the desire for property of his own. An intense educating force will inspire the wish for a home of his own, and awaken in him to be discontent with the teepee and the starving rations of the Indian camp in winter. This is what is needed to get the Indian out of the blanket and into trousers – trousers with a pocket in them – a pocket that aches to be filled with dollars."

Upon reading it again, she became livid, and brought it to the next family meeting. "I was a teacher!" May slammed the article on the table in front of her relatives. "We *never* had such outlandish ideas, like instilling greed into our own children, much less others."

Martha K. MacKenzie, Maysville's current teacher, picked up the story and began to read. "I've heard about the conditions on these reservations. Some of the Indian Agents withhold the food rations, keeping it, or even selling it while the people starve."

"They are inefficient and dishonest: nothing more than profiteers and pirates," Matthew said.

"I wish we could help them," Rebecca muttered.

"If the Bureau of Indian Affairs would take over," Joel explained, "things could get better fast. But as we saw in Denver, they won't get involved. They allow the government-appointed Indian agents to run things."

Falling Rock became angry in himself, hearing these things, but knew he could do nothing. Once again, he thanked the Great Spirit for allowing his people to live on native land under good conditions.

Chapter 7

WHEN BABIES COME

RICK Madison and Abe Wheeler were in the cow pasture watching the calves' birthings. It was important to be with first time heifers that often needed help. The mother was to lick off the calf and get it to suckle right away in order to get the colostrum, full of antibodies, within the first 24 hours, before the milk comes. If the mother is unable to do this, the cowboy will dry off the baby and get it to the teat. A warm, full tummy was the best defense against the early spring weather and cold wind. Unresponsive calves would suckle from a bottle.

The men were struggling with a breach. The head needed to be aligned with the feet, hooves pointing up. Rick tried turning the calf after pushing it back in, but the umbilical cord snapped. The baby took a breath while still inside, filled with water and died. Rick pulled out the corpse, turned white, and bent over, retching.

Abe let go of the head and came around to the back. "Oh, the poor thing." They laid the animal off to the side, and cleaned up the ground. The cow, with glazed-over eyes, didn't get up. "There's another one bawling," Abe said and walked that way.

"I'll go ask Mr. MacKenzie what to do," Rick went toward the barn.

Joel was helping Falling Rock with the horses that were having foals.

"Mr. MacKenzie, there's a still-born calf and the mother is not responding."

"She'll have to be put down," he answered sadly. "It doesn't happen very often, thank God."

"Then do I burn the bodies?"

"No. Put them in the wagon, take them up the hill and leave them. It helps keep predators off the property."

Rick took a pistol with him and performed the deed with tears in his eyes. "I'm so sorry," he cooed, then fired the gun. He brought the wagon over and put the dead calf in it, but needed help lifting the cow. Abe and Stan were there. As he drove up the hill he thought it was rather cruel to just leave them, but they were past caring. *I sure didn't bargain for this when I thought about being a cowboy.*

Falling Rock heard the shot, but was busy turning a foal. "Your horses," he told Joel, "are difficult."

"Sometimes they can be." He comforted the mare. One more strain and both fell into the hay.

"A colt," Falling Rock told Joel. "What was gunshot?"

"A still-born calf and sick cow."

Falling Rock nodded. Another mare delivered her filly without trouble. "Where's Rebecca? She likes to name the horses."

"Well," Joel paused to find the right words, "from what I hear…."

He hesitated and Falling Rock looked worried. "She's in her old bedroom in the big house, with Daniel, having her own baby."

Falling Rock quickly washed and ran to the house. "You can't go in," May stopped him at the door. "Her mother is in there with her." He heard a grown, then sat down at the table.

"Indian no have baby in bed," he said.

"That's our custom. That's how we do it." May handed him a cup of coffee. "Are you hungry?"

He looked at her with tired eyes. "Yes."

She served him some venison stew and bread. He ate slowly, listening for noises coming out of the bedroom.

"You should lie down for a while," May suggested. "First time babies often take a long time."

"I want to be there," he insisted.

May cracked open the door and asked Daniel if Falling Rock could come in.

"Only for a moment," he responded.

Ruth was wiping Rebecca's ashen face. Falling Rock could tell she was exhausted, but she was able to say, "Oh, Falling Rock." Then she groaned again.

"You'd better leave," Daniel said. "She will be fine."

Falling Rock kissed her forehead and left, lying down on the couch. The sun was setting when he woke up and looked at May who only shook her head.

Andrew, Burning Bear, and Rising Moon were at the table eating with Joel. Falling Rock paced as he heard the groans come faster. He went outside to pray.

Lighting a small pile of brush, he circled his arms in the air. "Great Spirit, you give life, I give thanks. You make baby for Rebecca and me. Help Rebecca now." He waved the smoke into the air once again, then stamped out the embers. Looking up, he saw the morning star and heard May call his name. He ran into the house where the bedroom door was open.

Daniel was cleaning up while Ruth attended to Rebecca.

"Falling Rock," Rebecca breathed weakly, "we have a girl." She tried to smile and lift the bundle to him. He took her and opened the top of the blanket and smiled.

"What should we call her?" Rebecca asked.

"Morning Star."

Rising Moon, now five, enjoyed holding Morning Star and helped care for her. May and her daughter, Sarah, would babysit so Falling Rock and Rebecca could go out riding.

May would often feel depressed at not being able to have any more children and have crying spells.

Her husband, Joseph comforted her as best he could. They would work together in the store and take buggy rides in the evening. Her spells grew less frequent with time.

Over the next ten years, Rebecca had three boys: Forest, River, and Canyon; and then another girl. "I want to name her Ruth Ann, after my mother."

Falling Rock agreed.

Chapter 8

SCHOOL

POPULATION continued to grow in Maysville. The town built a two-story schoolhouse, as folks were getting used to the Indians, and allowed the classes to be integrated.

The road into Maysville continued up the mountain, and children came down from mining camps to attend. Some even came up from Idaho Springs and other local areas. Martha K. MacKenzie taught 1st-6th grades downstairs, and a new teacher, Mr. Clifford Morgan taught 7th -12th grades upstairs. Andrew and Burning Bear had graduated from this class.

Two Negro couples came to town after the civil war, hearing of the opportunities the Indians had. The men worked in the stamp mill, grinding and sifting ores. Samuel and Miriam Jacobson became parents of a boy, Nathan and a girl, Olive. Chester and Buelah Boyd had two boys, Elijah and Josiah, and a baby girl, Esther. As soon as they were old enough, the children started school.

Three covered wagons came to town one day, each having a family, including children. The parents were interested in the school. Martha and Clifford met with them.

"We understand," said Mr. Smith, "that you have a very good school here."

"Thank you," Martha responded. "We try to have a wide variety of subjects the children are interested in."

"Do you really have mixed races here?" Mrs. Brown asked.

"We don't call them races," Martha explained. "You see, we are all part of *one* race, the human race, that God created."

"Well," Mr. Jones cleared his throat, "whatever you call them, *do* you have Indians and Negros going to school together with white children?"

"Yes." She smiled proudly.

"But how can that be?" Mrs. Jones asked.

Clifford spoke up. "You see, we value the individual student. All of them are given the opportunity and have ability to learn. Plus, we treasure their customs and ideals. For example, many of the Indians can speak their own language and English. They can practice their ceremonies while teaching others. It's a positive situation for all."

"But Negro *slaves?*" Mr. Jones persisted.

"Sir," Martha said, "the war ended many years ago. They are no longer slaves but free – people with lives, dreams and hopes, like everyone else."

"I don't think this may be the right school for us, after all," Mr. Smith concluded. "We will probably continue on to Utah."

"That's fine." Martha smiled. She and Clifford stood up to shake hands, but the men stepped back. Only the ladies dared touch Martha's fingertips.

Once the wagons were out of sight, Martha exhaled a sigh of relief. "Well, we can certainly see that prejudice is still rampant in this country."

"It's too bad," Clifford answered. "We have a much better way of life here."

Two men from the Colorado Board of Education came to Maysville, Howard Wolff and James Simeon. After introductions were made, they sat at a table with Martha and Clifford.

"We have a report here, Mrs. MacKenzie," Mr. Wolff started, "that you have operated a school in this area for a number of years."

"Yes, since 1865. I came here to teach school when another teacher had drowned."

"And after the Indian Charter was created in 1867, you have also allowed natives to attend?"

"Yes. They learn English and American law. They can read and write as well as any other child. Both groups of children help and teach each other."

"And how well is that working out?" Mr. Simeon asked.

"Extremely well," Clifford stated. "In fact, our two oldest boys, Andrew and Burning Bear, were our first graduates."

"Hmmm," Wolff grumbled. "What kind of curriculum do you use?"

They walked around the school while Martha showed them books and maps, chalkboards with assignments, and even musical instruments. Both teachers showed them lesson plans and explained how the different ages were taught. "We say the Pledge of Allegiance every day, pray and read a Bible verse. We also teach American Citizenship."

"That sounds good!" Simeon was delighted. "The Indians don't mind hearing the Bible?"

"It's another thing to learn," Clifford said. "We don't push religion on anyone, nor do we forbid them from what they know."

"But –" Wolff held up his hand. "Any student cannot legally graduate until he passes State Certification."

"That's fine," Martha conceded. "We will need to know how to obtain these tests and where to send in our reports."

"Of course," Simeon answered.

"One more thing, Mrs. MacKenzie, " Wolff continued. "We don't allow married women to teach school."

A knot of prejudice welled up inside her chest.

"We believe women should stay home and raise a family," Simeon clarified.

"Gentlemen," Martha tried to keep her voice patient," I came here as a single lady schoolteacher. I married here and have two fine sons. They are both in Mr. Morgan's class upstairs."

"That may well be, but it's still a rule of ours, *no married females may be schoolteachers*," Wolff insisted.

"Okay," she said and stepped behind Clifford, knowing that fighting now would do no good. Discretion was the better part of valor.

"Thank you, gentlemen, for coming.," Clifford said. He held out his hand; both accepted the offer of the handshake.

"And," Wolff continued, looking at Martha, "we have the right to come and inspect things any time we desire."

She nodded and lowered her eyes. The two men left.

"I never heard of such an ignorant position," Martha nearly screamed at Clifford. "Females are capable of doing a great number of things, including teaching *and* raising a family. Rebecca runs the ranch and has a family of six."

"I agree. We will have to research this ruling and see if there is a way to get around it."

Clifford prepared his report and presented it at a town board meeting where everyone was encouraged to participate. He began his search with the creation of the *Board of Education* in 1647. The passing of the 10th amendment in 1791 allowed each state to have educational authority.

Westward expansion beginning in 1803 spread Puritan ideals. Men, particularly farmers in rural areas, didn't want a pregnant woman teaching their children, even though farm children experienced animal husbandry first-hand. They thought it inappropriate to even *see* a woman in her *condition*, and thought she should remain at home. It could also become possible that the teacher would be unable to fulfill her term.

Clifford quoted one of many *rules:* "Women teachers who marry or engage in unseemly conduct will be dismissed immediately."

"But we're not farmers. We're ranchers and miners." Martha was adamant.

"Martha had our children when school wasn't even in session," Matthew stated. "There was no disruption of the term."

"I also faced that," Rebecca said, "when they wanted me to marry a farmer in Kentucky."

Falling Rock shook his head. *White man make much trouble for themselves.*

The town voted unanimously to keep Martha as a teacher. Everyone listed their names on a petition to present to the school board. Matthew drove Martha and Clifford in a carriage to Denver to appeal the decision. Mr. Wolff reluctantly accepted the document, presented it to the board, and the ruling was changed – *for this particular school only.*

It wasn't until the 1920s that married women teachers began to be generally accepted.

Chapter 9
HARGROVE

RICK Madison was working on a fence when a dude came to town riding a great white stallion, wearing a white 10-gallon hat ornamented with a silver band. His red kerchief tie clip was silver, shaped like a sword with loops on each side, a saddle in the middle between the blade and wooden handle, with a belt-buckle tip at the end of the wood. He had on a red, white and blue plaid shirt and furry chaps over his Levi Strauss blue jeans. His highly polished knee-high leather boots were etched with a feather and rope pattern and had silver toes. His long sideburns and handlebar moustache were black.

He rode up to Rick. "Howdy," he tipped his hat. "I'm Steven Hargrove here to start a rodeo circuit. Can you direct me to the owner?"

"That would be Rebecca MacKenzie," he replied and put down his tools. "Follow me." Rick stepped between the fence poles, going toward the barn. "Rebecca?" he called.

She came outside holding a mucking rake and took off her hat to wipe her brow, her auburn hair tumbling over her shoulders.

"This is Morgan Hargrove," Rick introduced. "He wants to talk to you about a rodeo."

"Thank you. Mr. Hargrove," she extended her hand for a quick shake, "please step down."

He removed his hat and was still considerably taller than Rebecca. "You have a beautiful place here." He flashed a toothy smile that Rebecca thought was flirtatious.

"So what is a rodeo?"

"It comes from Spanish cowboys, or vaqueros, at round-up time. It's a culmination of activities that folks do on ranches, a public exhibition of cowboy skills performed for prizes. For example, there's bareback and saddleback riding. This is where a cowboy rides a wild bronco and tries to stay on for a certain amount of time."

"We don't have any wild horses here. We breed thoroughbreds for sale. There are some that run on the ranges, but we don't catch or use them. Otherwise, we have work horses."

"I see." He put his hand on his chin. "There's also bull riding, calf roping, and wrangling steers."

"Our cattle operation is a side-line. We mostly sell the beef to the townspeople and miners. Of course we have to breed them to keep the herd going." She dipped her handkerchief in a bucket and wiped off her face and neck. "It all sounds very interesting and even fun. What would be our part?"

"You would supply an area of land. We would sponsor the event, bring the animals, and the prizes, which are donated by ranchers. We would bring a portable grandstand for the spectators. There would be entry and admission fees that we would share with you. You could even serve and sell refreshments, if you wanted to.

"The participants would come regularly to compete. That's where the circuit comes in. Eventually, we plan to have rodeos throughout the state as a showcase for our most treasured way of life, and the sports that are growing out of our Western culture." Falling Rock came and stood beside Rebecca.

Startled, Hargrove realized, "Oh, I know who you are now! I've heard about you. You're the people who live with Indians."

"Yes, this is my husband, Falling Rock." They shook hands.

"Well, talk about the rodeo with your staff, and I'll come back in a week."

The front door opened and Andrew's 15-year-old sister, Sarah, stepped out with a bucket full of scraps for the compost. She stopped and looked at the stranger, who smiled and waved his hat in a bow. Sarah blushed and ran inside.

"Goodbye for now," he told Rebecca and rode off.

Rebecca explained the rodeo details to Falling Rock. "What do you think?" she asked.

"I think it mean trouble. Strangers come. Things happen."

"I thought it might be good, especially for the children. There are several boys just in our family alone. Plus Morning Star is very good with the animals. It might be fun."

Falling Rock groaned without saying another word. He would have to take this up with the Great Spirit.

Chapter 10

RODEO EVENT

A LOVELY September day with aspen leaves in gold, clear sky, no wind, and 70 degrees ushered the circuit rodeo into town. Five acres of land south of the horse pasture had been cleared and fenced in a circle. A chute was built according to Steven Hargrove's specifications.

Rebecca and Falling Rock met Hargrove at the train at 10:00. He had a carload full of supplies, another of cattle, and another with the wild horses.

"It's nice to see you again, Steven" Rebecca extended her hand, and he flashed his smile. Falling Rock remained silent. "We have a great day for it," she continued. "I'm very excited."

Hargrove opened the first car and began pulling out wooden structures. "This is the seating – four chairs hooked together, folded up." He had 10 of them. Falling Rock helped him load the wagon.

Rebecca heard the animals snorting and stomping. "We can't leave them in there, can we? We have a corral you can use."

"That would be great!" Hargrove replied. "Maybe you can be in charge of that while we set up the arena."

Rick, Stan, and Abe assisted in unloading the stock. The cows seemed rather docile, so they took the horses out first. The livestock platform was designed to unload horses easily from a ramp directly into a temporary pen.

"Better stand back, Rebecca. I'll go first." Stan opened the door only wide enough to see activity. The wild horses were dangerously moving around in the boxcar. He was able to grab a lead rope, attached to a halter, and gently tried to coax the horse to the door. It was nervous and panting but moved slowly forward. Abe also grabbed the rope as Stan's hand reappeared, and the two of them were able to pull the horse out as Rick moved the door wide enough for it to pass. It resisted but soft words from all the cowboys eased his temperament. Rick closed the door partway, as Stan reached in for another Mustang.

Rebecca opened the gate and Abe took the horse to the pen. She spoke softly to it.

"Don't gentle him too much," Hargrove said. "He needs to be wild!" He and Falling Rock took the wagon to the arena. Falling Rock asked the MacKenzie boys to help Hargrove, and he went back to the horses.

The second horse was more ferocious, kicking, and snorting. It took three of them to hang onto the rope. "I wonder how Hargrove got these in here, in the first place," Rick said as he quickly shut the door. Falling Rock struggled with the rope, leading the horse into the pen. *Indians no do this way.*

"How are we going to get these to the arena?" Abe asked.

"We'll have to lead them, one at a time," Falling Rock said. "How many are there?"

"Three." Abe held onto the last horse and guided it into the enclosure.

The railroad yard was in-between the ranch and the arena, so it wasn't a very far walk to the corral, but it sure tested the strength of the men to hold on. Falling Rock took the lead ropes off the halters when they got there.

The ranch hands got on their own horses and herded the cattle to a second pen. There was one bull, two steers, two cows, and two calves.

"Wow," Stan said wiping his brow," that was enough work for one day!"

With the seating set up, Frederick and Matthew placed tables for the refreshments. Sarah came outside carrying two baskets with tablecloths, cups, and plates. A barrel of lemonade with ice was rolled into place.

Hargrove noticed Sarah, tipped his hat, smiling, and said, "Hello."

Sarah blushed and looked away.

"That's no way to behave," Rebecca scolded. "Mr. Hargrove is our guest, and you should make him feel welcome."

Sarah said a quiet hello without making eye contact.

Six cowboy contestants began riding in at noon. Rebecca was surprised to see Captain Anderson among them. "Hello captain," she greeted.

"It's just Jerry," he explained. "I mustered out of the army after the hearing you attended. I figured if we weren't going to enforce the law, there was no need for me to be there." His voice became bitter and he glared at Falling Rock. He was very uncomfortable with all the Indians in the area.

"I'm sorry you feel that way," Rebecca said and went to the house.

Inside was a flurry of activity. May, Sarah, Martha, and Star were packing food into baskets while the boys went outside. "I'm still not sure what to charge," Rebecca wondered. "Maybe a nickel each for everything?"

"That sounds easy," the women agreed, and took the baskets outside. Rising Moon was holding onto a squirming Ruth Ann and passed her to her mother.

A line had formed in front of Hargrove, who was enlisting the men in the events. The three MacKenzie ranch hands entered, along with the boys: Andrew and Burning Bear, Mark and Luke. Since Forest and River were under ten years old, they were not allowed to participate.

"Maybe next year," Rebecca told Falling Rock, "we should have our own rodeo for the children. We could have a BBQ and dancing too."

Falling Rock made no comment.

Star and Rising Moon served the refreshments. Daniel and Donna took seats next to them in case there were injuries. Falling Rock sat in the stands next to Rebecca, and Ruth Ann changed laps. Her father was able to settle her with gentle Indian words. Matthew located himself next to Martha and the new teacher, Clifford Morgan. Joseph and May sat together with Sarah and Frederick. Many townspeople and Indians turned up, along with a few strangers. Falling Rock watched them carefully. Once the seating filled, people stood around the outside of the arena.

The program started at 1:00. "Ladies and gentlemen, I am Steven Hargrove," he shouted through a brass-speaking trumpet. "Welcome to our first-ever circuit rodeo." The crowd applauded. "We have four events: bronc and bull riding, calf roping, and cow wrangling. There are refreshments being served by two pretty young ladies," he pointed to the girls, "Morning Star and Rising Moon. Food and drinks are just five cents each." More applause caused the girls to blush.

"Dr. Daniel MacKenzie is standing by, along with his lovely nurse, Donna." He pointed to them and Daniel waved his hat. "Hopefully, we won't need them.

"We have 13 contestants. So let's begin with broncs. The goal is to stay on the wild horse for 10 seconds."

The six *professional* cowboys were able to stay on the entire time and longer. MacKenzie ranch hands made it 7-8 seconds and the boys only 2-3. Burning Bear held on for nine seconds and won second place. The crowd roared in its applause.

Calf roping was the easiest event for all. Rick, Abe and Stan also did well with cow wrangling. And only the visiting cowboys rode the bull. Jerry Anderson fell off and broke his shoulder and collarbone.

The entire cache of refreshments was sold and the girls made $5.00.

Hargrove thanked everyone for coming and handed out ribbons and cash prizes. The overall winner, *Tex Brody*, won a small trophy.

Rebecca approached Hargrove and offered to buy the wild horses. "That would be great," he said with a sigh. "I really don't want the trouble of loading and unloading them again."

As many guests as could helped tear down everything and get it on the train. Meanwhile, Hargrove approached Sarah near a fence. "Well, how did you like it?"

"It was fine. Quite exciting at times."

Hargrove took her arm and tried to lead her behind the barn, but she resisted. "The best part is yet to come," he sneered.

"Stop it!" She screamed.

Burning Bear rushed out of the barn and knocked Hargrove to the ground.

"Don't touch her," Burning Bear shouted.

"How dare you," Hargrove retorted. He got out of the muck and mud, his white suit filthy. “I knew Indians would be trouble,” he snarled.

“The only trouble is you! Get out of here.”

Hargrove limped to this horse, his right leg injured. “We won’t be coming again,” he told Rebecca, and galloped away.

When the entire event was over, and everyone was gone, it was 7:00.

“Wow! What a day!” Rebecca stretched her shoulders and took a sleeping Ruth Ann from Star. Then they got the Hargrove story from Sarah and Burning Bear.

It was at that time Burning Bear declared his intentions for Sarah in front of everyone.

Chapter 11

CRIME

WHILE walking home from the rodeo with May and Sarah, Joseph noticed the store window was broken. "Stay here."

"Oh my," May gasped.

He looked through the window to see the inventory displays disheveled, and many items were missing.

He took his wife and daughter upstairs; the apartment was untouched. "I'll go get the sheriff," he said, and left.

"Mother, what's going on?" Sarah asked.

"The store has been vandalized," answered May. "Someone broke in and took what they wanted."

Sarah plopped down on the sofa, and May sat next to her. "What's happening today? That guy touched me, then this theft? I wish the rodeo wouldn't have come."

"Well, we sure can't change that, but we can determine how to respond to all this. How do you feel?"

Sarah trudged through a range of emotions and images. Her breathing became labored. "I feel dirty. No one has ever come close to me like that before. I'm afraid when I think of what could have happened."

"Darling, you did nothing wrong," May hugged her. "You were safe with everyone around. Burning Bear would protect you with his life."

"And what about that? Am I supposed to have feelings for him?"

"Slow down, dear. You are still very young. It will take time, if you are to develop any emotions. I'll draw you a bath, and then we'll go over to the big house."

Mike Sherman, the original sheriff of Maysville, mostly chased runaway animals, or answered calls at the ladies' boarding house and saloon. He was tall and well built, with black hair and sunburned face under his hat. The white line across the top of his forehead indicated many years working outside. He wasn't much for the paperwork end of things and usually hired someone else to do the reports for him.

He stood looking at the store damage, took off his hat, and ran his hand through his hair. "I was wondering if we'd get trouble from having strangers in town." He tested the front door, but it was still locked. "Is your family safe?" He looked at Joseph.

"Yes, May and Sarah are upstairs. Andrew is off with Burning Bear somewhere."

"Those boys are really good friends, aren't they?"

"Andrew was so disappointed when our baby boy died. He "adopted" Burning Bear as his brother. We don't know his exact age, so they decided to share the same birthday. They're 18 now, and just graduated from school."

"Wow!" Mike walked around the inside of the store with Joseph, stepping over broken glass, but not touching anything. Joseph described the missing items: tools, survival gear, dried food, and all the apples. "Looks like someone was trying to get away from something. I'll see if I can find any tracks. If I do, and they lead out of town; I'll need to contact the federal marshal."

Joseph and his brothers nailed boards in a crisscross pattern over the broken store window and door, hoping to keep further intruders out.

"Maybe you should come stay with us for awhile," Matthew offered. "I'm sure May doesn't feel safe upstairs."

"I'll ask her if she wants to," Joseph answered. "I hope they can find the culprit soon."

"I hope he hasn't fled too far," Frederick added.

Marshal Rick Sherman came to town and met with Mike. "Hello cousin," they greeted each other.

Rick and Mike looked almost identical except that Rick's hair was a light yellow-brown.

"I'm tracking a prisoner that escaped from the Colorado State Prison in Canon City," Rick explained. "I believe he was hiding out with the rodeo troupe."

"He's been here," Mike answered, and described the break-in at the store. "Rebecca MacKenzie reported a horse stolen from her barn."

"I guess I'm on the right trail, then."

Chapter 12

THE DEER AND THE BEAR

SOARING Eagle, one of the Indian survivors, was working in the horse pasture mending a fence when he heard an animal come crashing through the trees behind him. A deer bolted out with terrified eyes, and jumped the fence he was working on. He turned to watch it bound away when another animal lurched out of the forest. A huge black bear came straight toward him. He was able to fire his gun while still in the holster.

"What was that?" Rebecca let go of the hoof she was cleaning and looked at Falling Rock, who had already mounted the horse.

"Get Daniel," he ordered and rode off at a furious pace.

Daniel was treating some ill children in the big house when Rebecca ran in.

Panting, she said, "Trouble! Go out to the horse pasture."

When Daniel found Falling Rock, Soaring Eagle was severely injured, laying on the ground, moaning.

"I drove off bear," Falling Rock said, "but too late."

Daniel briefly examined the injured. “He’s still alive. Get a litter and some help.”

When he heard the shot, Rick Madison came, running. He and Rebecca were in the barn saddling horses when Falling Rock rushed in and grabbed a litter off the wall. “What is it?” Rebecca asked.

“Bear attack.” He rode off at breakneck speed, with Rick and Rebecca following him.

Daniel had managed to wrap some of the wounds to try to stop the bleeding. He and Rick carefully moved Soaring Eagle onto the litter.

“We should use wagon,” Falling Rock suggested.

“No time to get it hitched up,“ Daniel answered. “Go to the hospital,” he told Rebecca, “and tell Donna to prepare for emergency surgery. We’ll need oxygen, too.”

As Rebecca rode away, the men lifted the litter off the ground. They tied the ends where Soaring Eagle’s head was to each side of Daniel’s saddle. Rick and Falling Rock carried the litter handles with one hand while riding, holding the reins with the other, and slowly rode to town.

Jerry Anderson lay in a hospital bed with his neck and shoulder in a cast, his right arm held up in a sling. Donna was taking his vital signs when Rebecca rushed in. “What’s going on?” he asked.

“An accident,” she told Donna. “Daniel says get the operating room ready, with oxygen, too.”

Rebecca was assisting Donna when the men came in with the stretcher and laid it on the table.

“All of you leave,” Daniel insisted and Donna closed the door behind them.

It wasn’t long before Daniel came out and asked Jerry, “This man has lost a lot of blood. Would you be willing to give him a transfusion?"

"He looks like an Indian to me!"

"Yes, he is Soaring Eagle."

"Absolutely not!" was the curt response. Jerry turned his back to Daniel and faced the wall.

Daniel sighed and went back to the injured man. "Go get Falling Rock," he told Donna.

"Why would a bear attack a man like that?" Rebecca asked.

"See deer tracks," Falling Rock said. "Deer got away, but Soaring Eagle did not."

They went into the big house to tell the news to an anxious May. She stayed with the young children, and cooked, while others worked on the ranch. Rick took the horses to the barn to unsaddle them.

"It's odd," reflected May, "that a bear would chase a deer into town."

"It happens. I see." Falling Rock answered. "Hunger powerful force. Maybe protect young."

They all sat down at the table and prayed for Soaring Eagle and Jerry Anderson. Donna came in to get Falling Rock for the transfusion.

Falling Rock was put on the bed next to Jerry, who became even more disgruntled, turned his back and went to sleep. When he awoke, Falling Rock was gone, and a bundled mass of bandages and splints was breathing heavily beside him in the next bed.

Daniel came to the big house and collapsed in a chair.

"Well?" Rebecca prodded while handing him some coffee.

Daniel stared into the cup without taking a drink. "I don't know," he sighed. "If he lives, he will probably be crippled."

For the next two months, a surge of emotions ran through Jerry. First he was livid having to be laid up in a place right next to a *filthy Indian*. Then he was distressed when told it might take longer for his injuries to completely heal.

Jerry was taken outside, as often as possible, in a wheelchair, bundled up in blankets. The cool fall weather was shifting into winter. Children came daily to ask him about rodeos, the army, and anything else they could think of. Jerry didn't mind talking to the MacKenzies, but resisted questions from the Indian and Negro children.

Yet, as he saw their innocent faces and took note of their curiosity, the bigotry in his heart started to soften. He watched little ones of different colors playing in the snow in front of him without inhibitions. They built snowmen and soldiers, had snowball battles and weddings. Their unbounded joy became contagious.

As time passed, Jerry watched Soaring Eagle begin to recover. Bandages where changed frequently, then removed to show the shredded scars on his body. His labored breathing became easier.

Jerry's casts were finally cut off and Daniel released his patient. *Now what should I do,* he wondered.

Chapter 13

CHURCH

REVEREND Graham Tucker was polishing candlesticks in the Maysville Community Church, which was across the street from the school, when Jerry Anderson came cautiously through the door.

"Hello!" Tucker called, wiping his hands on his apron and hurrying down aisle. He met Anderson half way. "What brings you here?"

"I need to talk to someone. It seems all the MacKenzies have such decided ideas about things, and I have nothing in common with anyone else."

"Is that so? Let's sit down. Tell me about yourself."

"I was born in the south to a confederate family. After we lost the war, I enlisted in the Union army cavalry. I hated and wanted to hunt down every Negro and Indian person I could find.

"I actually came here to Maysville a few years ago to arrest Falling Rock and his people and march them to a reservation. But Joel MacKenzie was uncompromising in his protection of them. It made me begin to wonder if he was right, although I still pursued my military career.

"Then when I was able to apprehend Falling Rock, I had to put him in jail, instead of on a reservation, until a hearing was held. Falling Rock was released and I became so angry, I quit the army. I met Steve Hargrove and joined the rodeo circuit."

"That's very interesting," Tucker commented. "You seem to have some very deep emotions smoldering inside of you."

"That's what I want to talk about. As I lay in that hospital the last couple months, anger burned in my heart and mind. I saw many people coming and going to take care of the Indian. I heard them read the Bible to him and pray in the Indian language. Some would say *hello*, but I didn't offer conversation. Sometimes, someone would take me outside to get away.

"Then I saw the children, all together, playing – without any barriers. They didn't fight for position or possession. I wondered about that too."

"Children are born with only the will to survive. They have to learn how to hate from others, usually their family."

"Now, here I am, released from the hospital. I've been cared for and fed, and haven't even received a bill. I'm not sure what to do now."

"Hmm." Tucker nodded, his hand on his chin. He didn't speak for a few moments, and Anderson became uncomfortable. "May I call you Jerry," he finally asked. "I'm Graham. Let's take a walk."

There were deep snow piles beside cleared trails. The air was cold, but no wind was blowing; the sky overcast in gray. "Some people get depressed this time of year," Graham said, "with winter dragging on like this. But church attendance usually picks up when people aren't so busy!" He laughed, and Jerry forced a nervous smile.

"A country church sits at the center of every rural community,"

Graham continued. "And there's a heart within it, beating strong when people gather. They find peace through love and fellowship."

"I thought it was just a place to go, to practice religious activities."

"Oh, no, it's much more than that! We have a relationship with each other and God. We truly "love our neighbors," help whenever we can, and spread the gospel. You could benefit very much by coming to a meeting."

"First, I guess, I'll need a place to stay and get some work."

"I'd suggest seeing Rebecca MacKenzie. She's got plenty of work and there are cabins on her property."

Jerry frowned at the idea, but when no other offer was made, he thanked the Reverend and walked off.

Jerry's horse, Ranger, was boarded at the MacKenzie Ranch. He knew he would have to face Rebecca sooner or later. Falling Rock would probably be nearby too.

Chapter 14

THE BARN

REBECCA worked mostly indoors during the winter. She had to keep breeding records of all the horses, pay employees, and do all the bookkeeping. That, along with her six children, kept her quite busy. She was also teaching Rising Moon the basics of the business. Rebecca sent two three-year-old horses to the Denver Stockyards, although plans were being developed for a *stock show* that would showcase animals for ranchers and buyers.

Andrew, Burning Bear, and Falling Rock worked outside and in the barn with Abe, Rick, and Stan. Often, children would be around, playing and learning about animal care.

There's no place on the ranch more esteemed than the barn. Children learn the value of hard work and respect for life on the land. Character is often formed in the barn.

Morning Star was proficient with horses. She could ride, jump low fences, and rope calves. She also worked with the thoroughbred colts and fillies on *trust touch:* Beginning soon after birth by stroking and touching the foal in different areas while speaking softly. This allows the animal to gain confidence working with humans and make them worth more at the sale.

Andrew and Burning Bear were forking hay from a wagon to the cows in the pasture when Jerry walked up. "Is Missus MacKenzie around?"

"You mean my aunt Rebecca?" Andrew asked. "She's in the big house."

Jerry watched the scene for a moment. Men and boys were proficiently caring for the stock, cleaning, and mucking out the stalls, and a young girl was walking a horse on a lead rope. Everyone was doing something. He was amazed at the teamwork; no one got in another's way and help was given when needed. *Even the army didn't run that smooth.*

He knocked on the door of the big house, and heard, "Come in!"

Hesitating, he walked slowly into a room full of people, children of all ages, and two adult women.

May and Sarah were cooking and Rebecca was wrestling with a fussy Ruth Ann. She looked up when she heard the knock.

"Hello, Jerry," she greeted. "I've heard that Daniel has released you from the hospital."

"Yes." He suddenly felt shy and unable to speak.

"I bet you're looking for Ranger." He nodded. "He's out in the barn with the guys. You can go get him if you like."

"What do I owe you for boarding?"

"Oh, I didn't keep track of that. Feeding one more horse didn't make any difference. Ranger is a very nice animal and was pleasant to care for."

"Thank you." He didn't try to shake her hand before leaving. *Well, I guess I'm going to have to talk to Falling Rock.*

Forest, River, and Canyon, Falling Rock's three sons, were in the barn learning animal care. Forest knew how to do this, but he was patient while his younger brothers were learning.

Rick, Stan and Abe were behind the barn, building an addition.

Jerry walked up to Ranger in his stall. He began petting and talking to him.

Falling Rock came up beside him. "Nice horse."

"Thank you. He's a purebred Morgan from Virginia."

"You well now?"

"The doctor has released me. I thought I'd take Ranger out for a ride."

This was his chance. Jerry was free and he could ride away right now and never look back. He had some money in his pocket leftover from the rodeo. Ranger took him around the ranch and through town. Everything seemed so peaceful and orderly. There was no violence, shooting, or fighting. Only the noises of the stamp mill and other operations were noticeable. *I could have a good life here. But what about all those Indians and Negros?* He was shocked that he had even thought that. He rode around the area, down by the lake and rodeo arena, and saw the road leading south out of town.

Chapter 15

JERRY

GRAHAM Tucker met with Rebecca after church. "I've been praying for Jerry. He came to see me the other day."

"He's gone," Rebecca said flatly.

"Oh. He was asking me about working and living around here." He didn't offer the personal matters; they were confidential.

"I was thinking," continued Graham, "that with his command experience, and leadership qualities, he might make a good foreman for you. He seems like he'd be good with animals."

"I have been getting awfully busy, trying to run the ranch and manage the kids, and I never did replace Jonathan."

"It's something to consider," Graham encouraged, then they prayed together.

Jerry awoke on the floor, under a gambling table in Central City. His hands and face were sore from a fistfight he barely remembered, and his head throbbed from a hangover.

He muttered to himself, "and they call this *fun?*"

He lay there, unable to move, until a man came with a broom, poking him. "Gotta go, mister."

Jerry groaned and tried moving his legs. They began to twitch. He bent his elbows, putting his hands on the floor, and attempted to lift himself. Every movement was painful.

"C'mon mister, gotta get this place cleaned up." The janitor moved the table so Jerry could stand up.

"Thanks." Jerry's voice was hoarse.

"I think you have a bill at the bar."

Once settled, he brushed off his clothes with his hands and went outside. The bright sun nearly blinded him. He took off his hat and submerged his head in the horse trough, shaking it gently.

"Wow," he exclaimed, dripping. "I never want to do that again." With only $2 left, he went to the hotel for some food, and spent all of his money. *Now what?*

While his head was clearing, he began thinking about Maysville and the MacKenzie ranch. *Something Graham said* – he couldn't remember.

He got on Ranger and tried to find the exit out of town among the curved streets and dead ends. Each bar and gambling hall was raising a ruckus. He couldn't stand all the noise.

Weaving his way through Clear Creek Canyon, he found the road to Maysville and stopped. *Is this what I want to do?* With no money, home, or job, he considered if he could live among the Indian and Negro people. They actually didn't seem that different after all. He cinched his hat and turned Ranger north.

"Missus MacKenzie." Jerry stood at the door of the big house.

"Rebecca, *please!*"

"I'd like to talk to you, if you can spare the time."

"Of course." She invited him in to sit at the big table. Handing Ruth Ann to Rising Moon, she settled in a chair.

"What is it, Jerry?"

"I've been thinking about something the Reverend said." He paused and looked around the room. Only this table was free of clutter and debris. He saw a desk in a far corner stacked with papers and books. Toys and children seemed to fill the rest of the space; kids would often gather at the big house after school. Spoons and pots were banging.

"Rising Moon, please get them to do something quiet." She looked at Jerry with tired eyes.

"It seems you have a lot of work around here," he started, careful not to accuse or offend. "I thought maybe you might need some help."

"I always need help," she sighed. "Family work is so much harder than ranching! I've even got May and Sarah to help in the kitchen." She introduced the two ladies who never paused in their actions.

"I could be useful here," Jerry continued. "I have ranch experience growing up in Virginia, command training and organizational skills." He stopped when Ruth Ann began to cry.

"Take her out to her father," Rebecca told Rising Moon, "and tell Falling Rock to send in the boys for their naps."

She looked intently at Jerry. His steel blue eyes demanded respect. There were ripples of muscle under his shirt, and a peaceful, no, hopeful quality about his voice. "What I need," she grabbed a piece of paper and pencil off the floor, "is a ranch manager. Falling Rock and I have been taking care of this place since we lost our last foreman and my parents died."

"I'm sorry. Might I ask what happened?"

Rebecca looked off into the distance with tears forming in her eyes.

"I regret if I brought up an unhappy memory," Jerry apologized.

"No, it isn't unhappy." She took a heartfelt breath. "We found them asleep in each other's arms." Rebecca blinked away the distant look and dried her eyes.

"I just can't do it all anymore." She outlined duties of breeding and selling the horses and cattle, determining which horses to ship out, and making sure the men, and especially the boys, got the work done. "Plus, you'd have to do record keeping. I can help you get started and Rising Moon is learning it too. What do you think?"

"So far, I don't see anything I can't handle."

"Fine." She inhaled another deep breath. "You'll get a cabin, room and board, plus a salary, and a day off every week. You'll work with Falling Rock, not as his boss, but as his equal. You can discuss any situation with him and agree on a course of action. Can you also do this?"

Jerry stalled in his answer. This was the critical issue, wasn't it? He thought of his animosity toward Falling Rock, which seemed to be a fading memory. "Yes, I believe I can."

"Good." She gave a sigh of relief and they both stood up. Shaking hands, she said, "Falling Rock and I had already agreed on this, should you show up again." She grinned at him. "I'm glad you did. Go out and tell him it's all settled and have him show you around."

"Thank you, Missus –" She glared at him. "I mean, Rebecca." He picked up his hat and went outside as two little boys rushed in.

"Sarah, can you please watch the children? If you need help, go get Star. I've got to lie down for awhile."

Chapter 16

RECONCILED

MARSHAL Rick Sherman apprehended the convict who vandalized Joseph's store, and returned the stolen horse to Rebecca. Joseph was insured by a small, single-line mutual company in Denver, and was able to receive some restitution.

Since the offender was a prisoner, Sherman didn't think he'd be allowed to "work off" any of the damage, especially since he'd already tried to escape. The MacKenzie family all pitched in to recompense Joseph for everything he lost.

Matthew and Frederick assisted Joseph in rebuilding and restocking the store. Matthew's sons, Mark and Luke also helped. Mark liked working in the store, but Luke wanted to go to the Colorado School of Mines in Golden and become a geologist.

It was in those moments that Jerry understood teamwork, encouragement, and what it meant to be in a family. He watched children coming and going, growing and falling, constantly learning. Everyone, adults and kids alike, all accepted each other, like one big family. He was happy.

Once the marshal returned the inmate to prison, he came back to Maysville to begin an investigation of the two missing miners. He started by examining the cave at the waterfall.

Besides working with the horses, Falling Rock also liked being in the greenhouse. He'd never tasted vegetables before coming here, and especially enjoyed the green ones. He delighted in seeing the little plants grow, taking care of them, pulling out weeds, and watching for bugs.

Rebecca came in carrying Ruth Ann and looked at the plants. "Very nice," she commented. Ruth Ann started to fuss and squirm, reaching for her father. "She seems to want to be around you all the time."

"Yes," he took her and she settled down immediately. "We have kindred spirit."

"That's so wonderful," Rebecca cooed. "How are things working out with Jerry?"

"Him good man. Much nervous go away. Others like and respect him."

"I'm so glad! What a relief!"

Falling Rock set Ruth Ann in a box on the table beside him. She stared in amazement, watching him tend the plants.

After walking around the boxes, Rebecca said, "I think I'll go for a ride on Columbine. Want to come?"

"Yes." He washed his hands in a bucket and put on a special shirt with a large pocket in front that could hold the baby.

After informing the household of their plans, they rode off together. "It's so nice to get away like this," Rebecca breathed.

"Yes. You do too much. Your hair turning gold." He reached out and stroked loose strands. "You more pretty than ever."

She couldn't complain about the scar on her face, her wrinkles and tired eyes. She could just relish in his love.

Burning Bear and Andrew went riding frequently. They were together all the time, sharing a cabin on the property.

"I'm thinking of asking Sarah to go riding," Burning Bear said.

"She won't do it," Andrew snarled. "I don't think she's ever been on a horse. What's with you, anyway?"

"At my age, Indians think of marriage."

"Marriage! That's the last thing on my mind. I like being free!"

"I know. What about life? You'll do this forever?"

"I don't know," Andrew answered. "I haven't thought about anything else. But, Sarah? Really?"

"I like her." I see her working in the big house. She's quiet, works hard, helps with the children. I like her.

"Ugh," was all Andrew could say and spurred his horse.

Chapter 17

STOCK SHOW

ANDREW MacKenzie was proud to be Burning Bear's best man. He was glad to see his sister Sarah happy. He really couldn't remember her being happy, except maybe at her birthday. But today she and Burning Bear made a picturesque couple.

It didn't take Andrew long to realize he was lonely. He had spent the last 10 years or so constantly with Burning Bear. Of course he knew everyone in Maysville, but had never really become friendly with anyone else. Many girls eyed him as the most eligible bachelor in town, but he didn't pay them any attention. He decided to talk to Jerry Anderson.

He approached Jerry in the barn mucking out stalls. "With both you boys gone, I'll have to redistribute this work!" Jerry laughed and stood up to look at Andrew.

Andrew picked up a shovel and began filling the wheelbarrow. "I wanted to talk to you about something."

"Sure, let's go outside."

Morning Star was in the round pen working with a horse. The two men sat on the fence to watch her.

"What's on your mind, Andrew?"

"Now that Burning Bear is married I feel like I've lost my best friend. I don't know what to do next."

"Burning Bear is still around, it's just that his priorities have changed. As far as what to do next, there is a great big world out there." Jerry waved his hand across the mountaintops. "Some of it can be very good, but a lot more of it is very bad."

"Like what?"

"Well, for example, lingering in saloons is a waste of time, money and life. You learn to gamble and grow a desire for more. The more you win, the more you want. A lot of men become addicted. And if they're drinking, they can be very dangerous. There's also the women who loiter in saloons, not desirable by any means."

"I'm not interested in women."

Jerry nodded. "There's also a large amount of violence connected with drinking and gambling. Tempers become short and men get killed."

Andrew cringed at that thought.

"There's many more reasons people find for the killings: range wars, jealousy, greed."

Andrew began shaking his head.

Jerry continued, "You'd have to get a job to have a means of support and somewhere to live."

"Yeah, I guess I've got it made here. But I feel lonely and restless."

"I understand." Jerry rolled a cigarette and handed it to Andrew, who refused it. "There are many jobs out there. Some require college and others are just manual labor." He puffed the cigarette and blew circles into the air.

"Well, I'm used to manual labor."

"The best jobs, of course, would be in the city. Have you ever been to Denver?"

"We stayed there one winter when I little, but not since. I don't remember much."

"Maybe one of your uncles could take you there and show you around. You could see the different jobs, and where and how people live. There's an upper class, which concentrate on making money and seeking culture. The middle class workers have families and are usually happy. There are also poor people with crowded living conditions. The city is a wide variety of contradictions."

The more Andrew heard the more his stomach churned. He liked Maysville well enough. "What about somewhere else, not a city?"

"Most of the towns around here are mining camps. Not much different than this. You could go further west, say California, where they have orchards and farms."

Andrew sighed and thought for a while. He watched his younger cousin ride the colt. He admired her ability to work with the animals and enjoy being outside.

"I found what I was looking for here," Jerry said, "but you've had this all your life."

"Yeah. Well, thanks, Jerry." They jumped off the fence.

"You might talk with Reverend Tucker. He helped me quite a bit."

Andrew thought that would be futile. He didn't want to become a minister.

"Oh!" Jerry suddenly said. "There's also the Stock Show coming up soon. You might want to go to that."

Riding his horse, Spark, a reddish roan with yellow speckles, Andrew road around town looking carefully at the businesses and people. Girls going in and out of his father's store eyed him with scrutiny, then blushed and giggled.

Men working the stamp mill and other mining projects were sweaty and dirty, with big muscles bulging from their tight shirts.

He rode up to his uncle's business, *Maysville Guide and Outfitting,* leapt off his horse and went inside.

Matthew was standing at a map with a man who looked like a cowboy, showing him different areas for hunting. Frederick came out of the back room with an armful of rain slicks to hang up. Andrew went over to help him.

"What's going on, nephew?"

"Oh, nothing." Andrew sighed. "I don't know what to do now that Burning Bear is married."

"I take it you don't want to work in your father's store, or here?"

"No. I like being outside."

"Are you tired of the ranch?"

"Not really, but there's nothing *to do* here."

"Have you thought about what you *would* like to do?"

"I don't know. Jerry says there are lots of things outside this valley, but I'd have to get some kind of a job. I've never had a job where I've worked for someone else. We all work together here."

Frederick nodded his head as he arranged the slickers according to size. "Yes, we are a pretty small, tight-knit family community."

"Jerry suggested one of my uncles take me to Denver, or somewhere else. You're the only one not married."

"I could do that, sometime."

"Maybe to the Stock Show?"

'That's a good idea."

Andrew trudged upstairs to his parents' apartment. "Well," May said, "what brings you around here?"

"I don't know. I guess I miss you, and I'm lonely. I don't know what to do."

"I don't know what to do, either," May said, "now that the wedding is over. I guess I'll go back and work in the MacKenzie's big house again, and help your father."

"With Burning Bear around, I never realized I could get lonely."

"He won't be gone forever. Maybe *you* should get married."

"There's no girls in this town. They're all silly, like children."

May served dinner when Joseph came in. "The store's really getting busy now," he said. "I sure could use some help."

"I could help for a while," Andrew offered, "but that's not what I want to *do*."

After dinner, Andrew lay down on his old bed. "Lord, please give me some direction," he prayed and fell asleep.

Andrew was cutting calico for a customer when Rising Moon came in. "Andrew, your Aunt Rebecca wants to talk to you."

"Okay, tell her I'll come over when the store closes."

Falling Rock was holding Ruth Ann while Rebecca read to him out of a stock report, when Andrew came into the big house.

"Come and sit down," Rebecca invited.

"I go to greenhouse." Falling Rock left carrying Ruth Ann.

"What is it, Aunt Rebecca?"

"News has it that you've been thinking about leaving Maysville."

"I don't know yet. I don't know what I want to do."

"Consider this." Rebecca closed the booklet. "You know my heart's desire was always to have this ranch. And I feel much older now, especially after having children. Falling Rock is even older than I am."

Andrew shifted in his chair, anticipating what was coming; some difficult task or chore.

"And since you like being outdoors, and are very good with the animals, I'd like to make you my partner."

"Partner?" Andrew hadn't considered this.

"Jerry is very good at being the manager, but I'd like to keep the ranch in the family. This way, when the time comes, you will already own it. For now, you would share in the profits, more than just the wages you've received. Jerry and Rising Moon can teach you all about the technical business side, and you'll get to stay here in Maysville."

Andrew didn't speak; it was such a surprise to him.

"If you like, you can go do Denver with Frederick and think about my offer. I don't need a decision today."

How did Rebecca know he had talked to Frederick? Or that he was even considering leaving? *I guess you can't keep a secret in a small town.*

Chapter 18

TWO HORSES

TWO horses were loaded onto the train for shipment to Denver. Jerry, Frederick and Andrew took a wagon and met the animals at the stockyards and took them to the sale barn. Jerry told Andrew how to register them. The brand inspector, Bill recorded Rebecca's name for the MacKenzie Ranch, and gave Andrew a number for each. "The sale starts at 2:00 tomorrow," Bill said.

"Let's go get something to eat and find somewhere to stay," Jerry said.

The three men toured the mansions on Capitol Hill in Denver, and all the other neighborhoods. Andrew showed them the building where the family had stayed the winter of 1859-1860. It was now a hotel, and there was a room available for them to spend the night.

The next day, Andrew saw a girl walking in an opposite direction around the outside of the arena, with an older gentleman. She wore blue jeans, riding boots, a black Stetson hat, and a white silk blouse. Long black braids hung down her back. She made eye contact and they both smiled.

Andrew took the first horse into the arena. The auctioneer read the statistics: "This is a two-year-old filly, from the MacKenzie Ranch in Maysville, Colorado. She is a Kentucky thoroughbred with ground training, but has not been ridden. The bidding will start at $500."

The horse sold for $700 to the girl Andrew had seen. When they met near the pen, she said with a Spanish accent, "I only bought this horse because I wanted to meet you. I am Carlotta Mendoza. This is my father, Jose."

"Andrew MacKenzie." He shook hands with Jose first. A warm feeling came over Andrew when he touched Carlotta's hand.

Jose took the lead rope so he could put the horse in his wagon and said something in Spanish to Carlotta.

"We have purchased MacKenzie horses before," Carlotta continued. "They are excellent animals. We'd like to raise one to be a race horse."

"That's quite possible," Andrew answered. He felt shy talking to her.

"How come I've never seen you around here before?"

"This is my first time coming here."

"Oh." Carlotta felt like she was dragging the answers out of him. "What makes Maysville so special?"

"We're in the Rocky Mountains, about 10 miles west of Idaho Springs, in Clear Creek County. We have the best air, water and feed around."

"I see. I'd like to go there sometime. I haven't been to the mountains before."

"We have quite an extensive operation. We also raise workhorses and grow food for the townspeople. It actually started out as a mining camp."

"There's something else I've heard…." Her voice trailed off.

They began walking toward Jerry and Frederick who were waiting by a gate, and talking to each other.

"We have a fine school there with a lady teacher."

"That's it! It was something about the school. What else?"

"We have many differing cultures of people there. My family is from Scotland. My aunt Rebecca, who owns the ranch, married a native Arapaho Indian. Negro people came to live there after the Civil War. And a Chinese family just moved in to open a laundry."

"Wow! How do all these different people get along?"

"Quite well, in fact, because we all respect each other and their customs. We treat everyone equally, work together and help when needed.

"For example, my uncle Joe's store was vandalized, and the whole town pitched in to help him."

"That sounds very interesting. I've never heard of a community like that."

"You'd be welcome to come anytime." They met up with the two friends. "This is my uncle Frederick, and our ranch manager, Jerry. This is Carlotta Mendoza."

"Very glad to meet you," they said in unison.

"I'd better go check on my father now." She looked at Andrew and smiled, taking his hand." It's been pleasant talking with you, I hope to see you soon."

"Yes, that would be nice." Andrew blushed.

"She must like you," Jerry said after she walked away. "The other horse only sold for $600."

Frederick laughed and slapped Andrew on the back. "Yup," he said, "she sure got a good horse!"

Chapter 19
THE JOURNAL

GLORIA MacKenzie studied the chalkboard as her teacher, Mrs. Walker, wrote the assignment: *Family History*. "Now," she said turning around and brushing the chalk dust off her hands, "I know many of you children are descendants from the Arapaho Indians who originally lived here. And others," she looked at Gloria and smiled," come from the MacKenzies who first settled this area. But the rest of you may be immigrants from other countries or have just moved here from different areas. This project should be an interesting and fun trace of your genealogy. Some of you may not have much information, and that's okay. Do some research and come up with the best you can."

Gloria was thrilled with the project. This was 1960, exactly 100 years since her ancestors first arrived here. She knew there were several books in the library about the railroad and mining history of Maysville, but what she was after was her great-grandmother's journal, Rebecca's story of the adventure.

Gloria's cousin, Selah met her after class. "Oh, isn't this exciting?"

Selah's enthusiasm was contagious. "Most of our story should be the same since we're related. Maybe we can work on this together?"

"Yes," Gloria agreed, "but the first thing we have to do is find Rebecca's journal. It tells everything."

"Really? I think I've heard of a journal, but I don't know anything about it."

"Grandmother Rising Moon will know where it is."

The girls ran home from school and were out of breath when they burst into the kitchen of the big house to find a small, old woman sitting at the table shelling peas and humming quietly.

"Grandmother Rising Moon!" they said in unison.

"My goodness, what is it?" She pushed the bowl aside to look at them. "Do you need some water?"

"No, we're okay," said Gloria. "We're just excited."

"We have a new school project," Selah began to explain.

"Yes. We are to make a report about our family history our family history," Gloria blurted. "We need to find Rebecca's journal."

"I see," murmured Rising Moon. "That is exciting. I haven't seen that book in years."

"It should be around somewhere." Selah was hopeful.

"Maybe in the attic?" Gloria offered.

"Maybe...." Rising Moon pushed herself up and stood. "Maybe there or in the stables. She did a lot of her writing with the horses."

"Let's try the attic first," Gloria said, and both girls got up. "Do you remember what it looked like?"

"Hmmm...." Rising Moon closed her eyes to visualize the elusive book. "I think it was red velvet with gold leaf pages. Her brother Daniel gave it to her for her birthday."

"Thanks!" the girls said and gently hugged their grandmother.

"Wait! You'll need a flashlight. There is no electricity in the attic."

The girls cautiously climbed the narrow stairway until they came to a closed door. Turning on the flashlight, Gloria held her breath while pushing open the door. A cloud of dusty, stale air rushed out that was fanned away before stepping inside. "Over there," said Gloria. She pointed to a small window shedding a little bit of light. There were tall items covered in cobwebs they didn't recognize, and stacks of boxes along the walls.

Gloria knew what she was looking for: a trunk – one that Rebecca's grandmother had given to her before she came out west. They carefully walked along narrow beams to keep from stumbling. "Looks like you could fall right through the floor," Selah said.

As they reached the window, there was the trunk. Using a damp rag Gloria had brought along with her, she painstakingly cleaned the case before opening it. Selah dried it off with a second cloth. The leather hinges cracked and crumbled as they carefully lifted the cover.

There it was, right on top: a faded red-velvet journal with embossed gold lettering *Rebecca Ruth MacKenzie.* Gloria tenderly removed it and wrapped it in a small towel. They closed the lid and went downstairs.

Sitting at the table, they let the book fall open. The page was yellowed, and had writing on it. "Look," Selah pointed to a watermark on the words *broken heart.*

Gloria gently closed the journal, the velvet staining her fingers. "Let's start on this tomorrow," she told Selah. "Bring some paper and a pencil."

Gloria couldn't imagine the hardships and difficulties of traveling cross-country in an open wagon. And then, to lose your horse, your very best friend in the whole world.

Selah and Gloria sat at the picnic table under a shade tree. "Let's begin," Gloria said opening the book cover. "Look at this."

She showed Selah a hand-written genealogy. "Write this down."

Shawn and Bridgette MacKenzie came to America from Scotland in 1810 with son, Joel. They lived in New York.

Joel married Ruth Ann McKenna in 1830; they lived in Kentucky. They had four sons and one daughter.

Joseph married May in 1852. They had one son, Andrew, and one daughter Sarah.

Daniel became a medical doctor in 1854. He married Donna in 1870.

Matthew married Martha Kauffman in 1856. They had twin sons, Mark and Luke.

Frederick was 21 in 1858. He never married.

Rebecca Ruth MacKenzie was 21 in 1861. She married Arapaho Indian Falling Rock and adopted orphan, Rising Moon. They had a daughter, Morning Star; three sons, Forest, River, and Canyon; then another daughter, Ruth Ann.

Two of the brothers, River and Canyon, married two sisters, Greta and Freda Swenson, in a double wedding. They each had a girl born on the same day, Gloria and Selah.

"That's where it stops," Gloria said. "She must have seen us before she died."

"Wow," Selah said softly. "I guess we'll have to read the whole book to find out what happened."

They took turns reading the journal out loud. The story didn't give much information about the family history, except why they moved from Kentucky. Joel's wife, Ruth, had consumption.

They did their library research and wrote a joint report. Then they shared it with Rising Moon.

"Grandmother Rising Moon," Gloria said, "you were there, weren't you?"

"Yes, my child. I lived through it all."

Printed in the United States
by Baker & Taylor Publisher Services